For the members of the Mac's
Book Club Show Book Club —MB

For my grandparents,
Bill and Anne —GP

VIKING

An imprint of Penguin Random House LLC, New York

First published in the United States of America by Viking,
an imprint of Penguin Random House LLC, 2020

Visit us online at penguinrandomhouse.com

LIBRARY OF CONGRESS CATALOGING-IN-PUBLICATION DATA IS AVAILABLE
ISBN 9780593113981

Manufactured in China
Book design by Greg Pizzoli and Jim Hoover   Set in Clarion MT Pro

10   9   8   7   6   5   4   3   2   1

CK
AND
SANTA

Mac Barnett & Greg Pizzoli

Viking

1.

SANTA

This is Santa.

He lives in the snow.

He makes toys
and makes lists.

TO DO
• PLANES
• TRAINS
• AUTO-
   MOBILES

And he gives people gifts.

Look!

He has two lists.

One is GOOD.

One is BAD.

If you're on the GOOD list,
you will get gifts.

Gifts such as toys.
Toys make very
good gifts.

If you're on the BAD list, you will get coal.

Coal is not fun.

It's not really a gift.

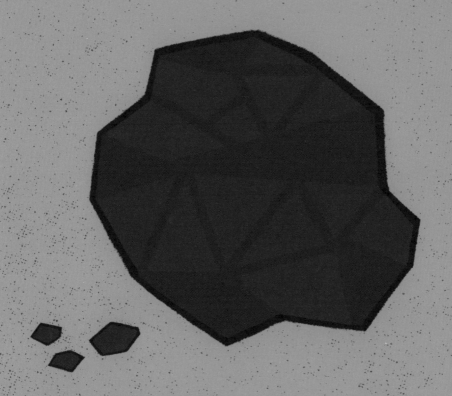

Hey, Santa!
Can we take a
look at your lists?

GOOD
~~BRYAN~~
~~TAYLOR~~
HENRY
~~KAY~~
~~JOHN~~
~~SARAH~~
SOPHIA
KATE
~~ELLIE~~
ARIEL
EMILY
KEN
TAMAR
~~JIM~~
~~BEN~~
THE
LADY
REX

The GOOD list says
THE LADY and REX.

The BAD list says JACK.

Oh.
Jack won't like that.

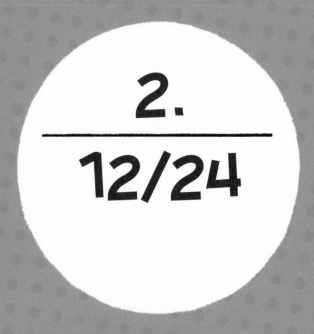

2.

12/24

This is Jack.

He lives with
the Lady.

He sleeps every night
in a bed next to Rex's.

What's that in
Jack's hand?

It looks like a list.

It's Jack's Wish List!
It's a list full of gifts!

Let's see what Jack wants.

We'll sneak up while he
sleeps and peek at his list.

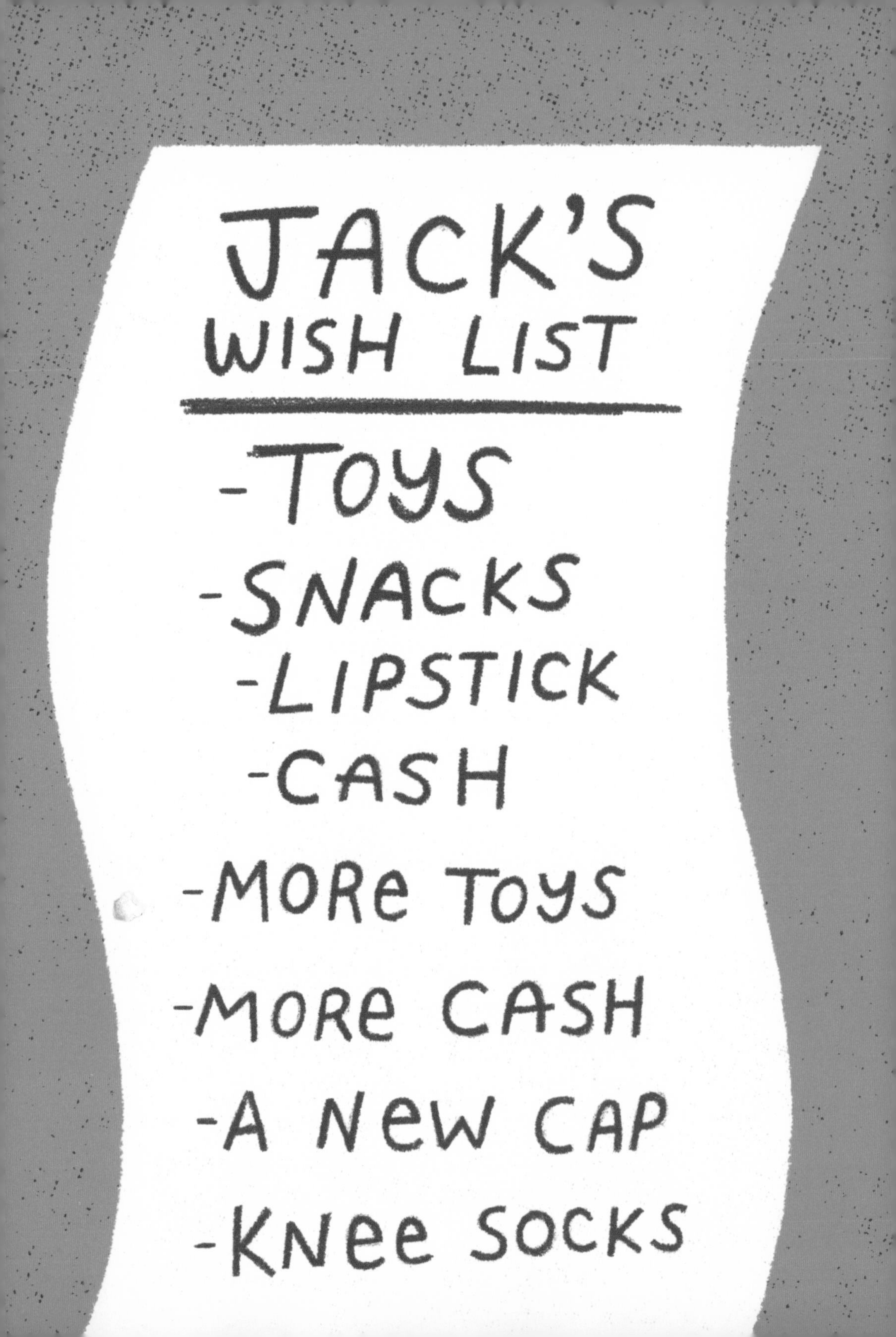

JACK'S
WISH LIST

- TOYS
- SNACKS
- LIPSTICK
- CASH

- MORE TOYS

- MORE CASH

- A NEW CAP

- KNEE SOCKS

-A BAT
(FOR BASEBALL)
-A BAT
(FOR A PET)
-A CHESS SET
-ALL THE TOYS
AT THE STORE
-ALL THE CASH
IN THE BANK
-A BAG
(FOR MY TOYS)
-A BAG
(FOR MY CASH)

Oh boy.
That's a long list.

But look at Jack sleep.

He's so sweet
when he sleeps.

When Santa comes
here tonight, he will
see Jack asleep.

He will see Jack is nice.

He will see Jack is sweet.

He will see Jack is good.

He'll see Jack is the best!

Maybe then he will give Jack
some things on his list.

- A BAT
(FOR BASEBALL)
- A BAT
(FOR A PET)
- A CHESS SET
AT THE STORE
- ALL THE TOYS
IN THE BANK
- ALL THE CASH
- A BAG
(FOR MY TOYS)
- A BAG
(FOR MY CASH)

Do you hear that?

It's bells!

That's Santa's sled!

Do you hear those footsteps?
That's him on the roof!
Do you hear—

CRASH!

What was that?
Oh no!

Santa is caught in a trap!

Who would set such a trap?

JACK!

3.

SANTA TRAP

This is not good.

In fact, this is bad.
Jack, you've been bad.

This is the worst.

Jack, you don't get
to go in that sack!

There is a big
box for the Lady.

There is a big
box for Rex.

There is no
box for Jack.

Jack.

Oh, Jack.

Santa, what did Jack
do that's so bad?

Other than that trap.

OK, besides that.

Right, well, there's that.

Oh yeah, that was bad.

Yeah, so was that.

But, Santa, can't you
just let Jack be Jack?

Jack gets Santa down.

Jack gives Santa
some snacks.

He gives Santa
a kiss.

Santa takes off his hat.

He pulls out a small box.

The tag says "For Jack"!

And with that, Santa's gone.

Unwrap that box, Jack!

Oh. Coal.

That's cold, man.

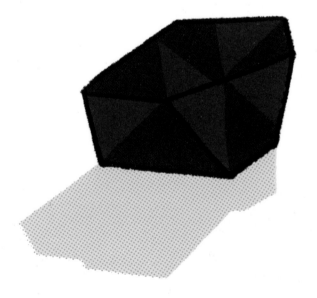

4.

A
FEAST

The Lady wakes up
and opens her gift.

So does Rex.

But where's Jack?
And what smells
like fire?

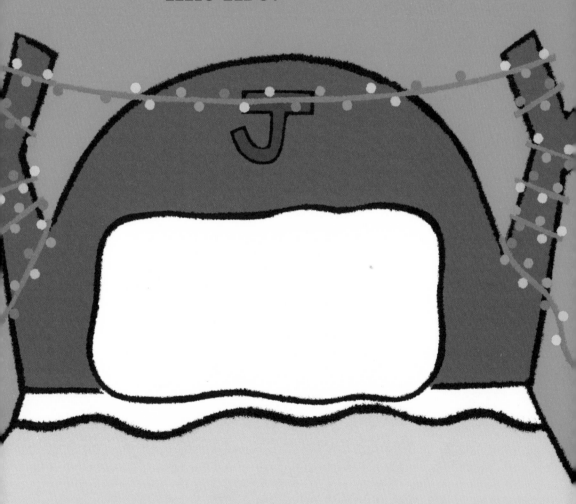

Oh no.
Jack! Jack!

Well, look at that.
Grilled cheese!

Jack used the coal
to grill up a feast!

A feast for the Lady.

And a feast for Rex.

And all the ladies
in town!

There's a long line.
Jack grills food for them all.

That's good, Jack!
You're a good Jack!

There's one grilled
cheese left.
And it's the end
of the line.

Who's that, at the back?

It's Santa!

He's back!

"Jack," Santa says.

"I was wrong. You're not bad."

"I smelled this great
feast from the sky.

I saw you share.
And I smiled.

I am here just in time!
I love grilled cheese.

And that looks like
the last one!"

JACK!

Well, I don't
blame you, Jack.

Not for that.

Not one bit.

THE
END

HOW TO DRAW...
SANTA!

IF YOU WANT MORE JACK, READ:

HI, JACK!

Mac Barnett & Greg Pizzoli

A JACK BOOK

JACK BLASTS OFF!

Mac Barnett & Greg Pizzoli

A JACK BOOK

JACK GOES WEST

Mac Barnett & Greg Pizzoli

JACK AT BAT

Mac Barnett & Greg Pizzoli

A JACK BOOK

TOO MANY JACKS

Mac Barnett & Greg Pizzoli

A JACK BOOK

JACK AT THE ZOO

Mac Barnett & Greg Pizzoli